Fairytales Retold
The Twelve Brothers

Fairytales Retold The Twelve Brothers

Avril Sabine

Cracked Acorn Productions Australia

Fairytales Retold: The Twelve Brothers

Published by

Cracked Acorn Productions

PO Box 1365

Gympie, Queensland 4570

Australia

978-1-925131-08-6 (Kindle)

978-1-925941-17-3 (EPUB)

978-1-925131-44-4 (Large Type Print)

Genre: Fairytales Retold Short Story

Cover design by Caitlyn Petersen

When Princess Ilsa discovers that she has twelve older brothers she is determined to meet them. Their father has declared they should die and, unknowingly, Ilsa places them in mortal danger by seeking them out.

*

People have been telling stories since the beginning of time. Fairytales, folklore, myths and legends are among some of the stories that have been told over and over through the centuries. The basic story remains the same, but each storyteller adds their own style, sometimes adding something unique to the tale.

*

This story was written by an Australian author using Australian spelling.

The Twelve Brothers

Ilsa walked along the castle corridor, black hair piled elaborately on her head, her dress far too elegant for morning wear. It had been laid out for her this morning and could only mean one thing. She headed towards the gardens hoping to avoid yet another torturous day. She froze. It was too late. Ahead and around a corner, she heard voices. It was her father and Prince Abelard, her fiancé.

Gathering up her skirts, she spun, hurrying away in the opposite direction. When she reached her room, she turned the door handle, stopping when it occurred to her that it was the first place they'd look. Her hand fell to her side. It had only been three days since he'd last visited. Not long enough.

Looking around, she tried to think of where she could go. Hearing their voices drift towards her, she continued along the corridor and turned at the next intersection, taking random turns until she found herself in the old part of the castle. Her steps slowed as she wondered if she should turn back. She'd been told never to enter the old section, that it was dangerous and in disrepair. But this part seemed fine. The thought of having to listen to Prince Abelard talk endlessly about what he expected from his future wife, kept her moving. Their fathers had betrothed them at her birth, ending a lengthy war. When she turned eighteen next year, they'd be married. It was the last thing in the world she wanted, but what choice did she have?

Pushing the thought from her mind, Ilsa opened one of the doors along the dusty corridor. Sunlight struggled through the window trying to banish the shadows that filled the bedroom. Cobwebs and dust swathed the hangings on the four-poster bed, making the velvet look more grey than green. At the foot of the bed was a carved timber chest that caught Ilsa's attention. She'd expected fallen walls, gaping floors and precarious piles of rubble. There was none of that. Moving close to the chest, she ran a hand across the carvings, dust clinging to her fingers. Why hadn't she been allowed to enter the old section? She slowly lifted the lid of the chest.

Frowning, she brushed the dust from her fingers before she pulled out one of the shirts that were neatly folded. Herbs were strewn amongst the fine linen, falling into the chest as she shook out the garment. She withdrew shirt after shirt, each as finely made as the last. In all, there were twelve. Running her fingers over the material, she stared at the shirts. Where had they come from? Who owned them? She didn't have a clue, but she was determined to find out, even if it meant getting into trouble for being in the old part of the castle. Returning all but the smallest shirt to the chest, Ilsa wondered if it was safe to look for her mother. Surely her father and Prince Abelard would have finished searching the castle for her and be looking in the gardens by now. Several minutes passed before she convinced herself to leave her dusty sanctuary.

It took nearly an hour to find her mother, who was in the kitchen discussing the evening menu with the cook. She turned to Ilsa with a smile. Her once black hair was now completely grey, plaited around her head and held in place with pearl pins. "Your father was in here looking for you."

Instead of commenting, Ilsa held out the shirt she'd found. "Who owns this?"

Her mother's smile disappeared as she took the shirt, bunching the fabric in her hand, pressing the garment against her chest. "Where did you find this?"

"I counted twelve. All of them different sizes. Who owned them?"

"I haven't time for this, Ilsa. Go and find your father. Prince Abelard has travelled half a day to spend time with you." She left the kitchen.

Ilsa fell into step beside her. "Do you know who owned them? And who put them in that room?"

Her mother stopped and faced her. "You've been in the old part of the castle. What have you been told about going in there?"

"Why won't you tell me who owned them? And don't try and tell me you know nothing about them because you knew exactly where they were without me telling you."

Her mother stared at her a moment longer before she turned away and continued along the corridor.

Ilsa persisted, asking numerous

questions until her mother said, "Why can't you forget all about them? Please, Ilsa."

"Tell me and I will."

"They belonged to your brothers."

Ilsa played the words over and over again in her mind, but still they made no sense. "My what?"

"Your brothers. There are twelve of them."

"Where are they?" And why had no one ever told her about them?

Her mother's gaze dropped to the shirt in her hands. "They left home before you were born."

"Why?"

"You said you'd forget about them if I told you."

"But you haven't told me anything." Frustration drove Ilsa to continue questioning her mother who eventually gave in again.

"Your father was determined to end the war between our country and Prince Abelard's. He told me that if we had a daughter he'd kill our sons so you could inherit. He wanted to betroth you to our enemy to bring about peace and end the senseless bloodshed."

Again Ilsa struggled to make sense of her mother's words. "I have brothers?"

Her mother nodded.

"Where did they go?"

"I don't know. I've heard the occasional rumour that they might be living in the forest south of here, but I don't know for certain. I don't want to know and I don't want to encourage the rumours. I want them to be safe."

"How could Father even think of killing them? His own sons."

"To save the lives of countless others. You don't know what war is like, Ilsa. We were losing. It was only a matter of time before not only our people died, but our children and ourselves. One day you will have to make the same hard choices."

"Never." She had brothers? It seemed impossible. How could her father have thought killing them was a solution? "I want to meet them."

"I've already said I don't know where they are. You're not to leave the castle. I won't lose you too." She wrapped her arms around Ilsa, drawing her close, the shirt still bunched up in her hand.

Ilsa smothered the urge to argue. She'd wait till night then sneak out of the castle and see if she could find her brothers. Surely it couldn't be that difficult. Twelve men all living together would have to have been noticed by someone.

She drew away from her mother, trying to take the shirt. "Can I at least have this?"

Her mother held onto it a moment longer before she let Ilsa take it from her. "Prince Abelard will probably be in the gardens by now. You need to spend some time with him. Don't let this all be for nothing."

Ilsa again resisted the urge to argue, giving a single nod instead. She strode away, leaving the shirt in her bedroom before she reluctantly went to the gardens to find Prince Abelard. The hours she spent with him in the gardens were as tedious as she'd expected, with dinner being little better. She escaped to her room as soon as the meal ended, claiming tiredness. But she lay awake in her bed, staring into the dark. Waiting for the castle to quieten around her, she wished she'd thought to ask why she'd been told the old section was too dangerous to enter. She could only think it was because evidence of her brothers' existence had been hidden away in there.

When she thought enough time had passed, she rose from her bed. Lighting a candle she threw a change of clothes, some money and jewellery and the shirt into a bag. Blowing out the candle she slipped through the castle, stopping in the kitchen for food to take with her, before stepping into the cool night air.

It took her longer than she expected to saddle her horse, but she finally led her mare to the side gate of the castle grounds. Sliding back the bolt, she slipped out of the heavy wooden gate, quietly closing it behind her. She was unable to do anything about locking it. Mounting her horse, she turned south and headed for the forest that was several hours from the castle.

Before sunrise, Ilsa found herself nodding off and decided to stop and rest. She had no idea how long she had slept, curled up against the base of a large tree, but the sun was high in the sky when the sound of hounds woke her. For a moment she didn't have a clue where she was, then it came back to her. Scrambling to her feet, she tightened the girth of the saddle and swung up onto her horse.

The sounds of barking came closer and she urged the horse forward, leaning over her neck. "Come on." She glanced over her shoulder, but although she could hear the hounds, she still couldn't see anyone. She shouldn't have slept so long. "Hurry, girl."

Ahead was a stream and Ilsa, recalling a story her father had once told about losing a stag that had followed the stream, urged her horse into it. She followed it upstream, in the direction of the wind. She would go south again when she'd lost the hunters.

It was hours before she could no longer hear the hounds. When the forest had been quiet for a few hours, she turned her mount south again. By the time the sun was setting she still hadn't seen any sign of people. Dismounting, Ilsa tied her horse to a tree. After eating some of the food she'd brought with her she fell into an exhausted sleep, her body aching from the hours of riding.

All night different sounds dragged her from sleep. She'd then lay awake, ready to flee if necessary. When she remained safe, she'd drift off to sleep again. By morning she was tired and sore and wondering at the impossibility of her task. Breaking some bread from the loaf she'd pilfered from the kitchen, she ate it as she rode, her gaze searching the forest. Late morning, she heard a different sound and headed towards it.

As it grew louder, she dismounted, tying up her horse so she could creep closer. Peering past a tree trunk, she saw a group of men chopping down a tree. Counting them, she found eleven. Disappointment hit her and she turned away. She was tired, her muscles ached and exhaustion made her want to curl up under the nearest tree and sleep for a week.

"All right you lot. Come and get your food while it's hot. The timber will wait, the food won't."

Ilsa turned to see who had spoken. Another young man had joined the woodcutters, carrying a large pot of stew that he sat on a stump. As the men lined up in front of him, holding bowls, he ladled out generous helpings.

"Why didn't you bring bread, Benjamin?" one of the men asked.

"Because I spent the morning hunting. Did you want meat in your stew or bread?" Benjamin asked.

"Both. You need to be more organised. It's not like taking care of the house is a hard job."

Benjamin snorted. "I'd like to see one of you lot try. You all eat so much I spend most of my day cooking."

Ilsa watched in fascination as the men ate and talked. Some had sandy brown hair, some dark brown and a couple had black hair. Almost half of them sported beards and their ages seemed to range from early twenties to about forty. Were these her brothers? There were twelve of them. Again she counted. Twelve. Should she step out of the trees and ask them? Her gaze was drawn to each man. One of them seemed to have a permanent frown. What if they didn't want to see her? Her brothers had been princes until she'd been born. And worse yet, what if they weren't her brothers?

The youngest gathered up the bowls, putting them into his now empty pot and heading away from the group of men who had returned to cutting trees. Ilsa hesitated a moment before she dashed through the trees, untied her horse and hurried after him. The sound of the woodcutters grew quieter as they continued south.

Benjamin stopped and looked around. "Is anyone there?"

Ilsa slipped behind a tree, holding her breath.

"Anyone?"

Should she step forward? Her hand tightened on her reins.

"Fredrick, if you're playing some kind of trick again you'll be sorry." Benjamin looked around one last time before he turned away and started along the track that wound its way through the forest.

Tying her horse to the tree, Ilsa forced herself to step onto the track and hurry after him. "It's not Fredrick."

Benjamin spun to face her. "Who are you?"

"I'm looking for my brothers. I'm Ilsa."

The pot dropped from his hand, landing on the ground with a rattling thump. "The princess?"

She nodded.

"Princess Ilsa?" Benjamin took a step forward, the pot left behind. "My sister?"

Again she nodded. She didn't have a clue what to say to him. Why hadn't she figured out something to say? She'd been so focused on finding them she hadn't even thought about this moment.

Benjamin took one more step towards her before he looked around, stepping backwards. "How far away are they?"

Ilsa frowned. "Who?"

"Whoever was sent to kill us this time."

"No one. I found your shirts and made our mother tell me all about you." She rummaged in her bag, taking out the shirt she'd brought with her.

Benjamin's gaze was drawn to the shirt and he took a single step forward. He stretched out his hand as if he was close enough to take the shirt, but then quickly drew it back. "Are you certain? There's no one coming for us? We don't have to move again?"

Ilsa shook her head, taking several steps forward, still holding out the shirt.

"Then why are you here?"

She began to say it was because she had wanted to meet them. "I just wanted..." her voice trailed off and she shook her head as panic hit her at the thought of her future. "Don't make me go back there, please. I know I should marry him, but I can't. I'm a princess, I should be able to marry him for the greater good. I should want peace for my people." She took several more steps forward until she was right in front of her brother. "Please. Don't make me go back."

Benjamin reached out, his fingers lightly grazing her cheek, before he rested his hand on her shoulder, his fingers momentarily tightening. "I never thought to see you. Ever."

"Please."

"I thought I'd hate you. That I'd want to kill you for stealing our lives from us. For forcing us to run and hide and keep on running. I was six years old when I found our mother crying and kept pestering her until she told me what our father had planned. I even made her show me the twelve coffins that had been made for us. The smallest one was lined with white silk. It sat there with the lid open, waiting for me."

"How did you get away?" She reached up, to rest her hand on his, her arm crossing her chest.

"It was Aaron. He was only twenty-one and our father was grooming him to be the next king. He found me hiding in the gardens when no one else could. He swore he'd save us. That we'd make our own way in the world. He's the one you have to ask if you can stay. Without Aaron none of us would have survived the first year."

"What happened the first year?"

"Assassins."

Ilsa's throat tightened. "You were so little."

"Fredrick was only two years older than me. Our father didn't care how old any of us were. Only that we died so you could inherit. I should hate you." His hand, still on her shoulder, tightened.

"I didn't know. I never wanted any of it." How could she convince him?

He drew his hand away from her shoulder. "It's not me you should be talking to. I never would have been king. Aaron is next in line."

"What can I say to convince him?"

Benjamin shrugged. "If you were dead, he could inherit. Our father would have no choice other than to accept us all back. He needs an heir."

Fear slid through her. "Please. Help me convince him. I can't go back there. I can't live that life." She took a step forward, reaching for Benjamin's hand with both of hers. She felt the calluses on his work worn hand. "Benjamin. Please. I have no one else to turn to."

He stared down at her a moment longer, drawing his hand away from hers. "I can't promise you anything. I'll convince him to listen to you. The rest is up to you."

Ilsa nodded.

"Come back to our house then. You might as well make yourself useful while we wait for our brothers to finish work for the day." Benjamin collected the pot and started along the track.

Ilsa shoved the shirt in her bag and hurried off to fetch her horse, mounting it so she could catch up with Benjamin who hadn't waited for her.

When they arrived at the house, Benjamin put her horse in the stable at the side of the house before he set her to cleaning up the kitchen. He watched her for several minutes before he turned away to prepare vegetables to go with the venison he was roasting in the large wood oven that took up most of one wall of the kitchen.

Once the kitchen was clean, Ilsa wandered through the rest of the house, telling Benjamin she'd tidy up when all she really wanted was to see where her brothers lived. It was nothing like the castle they'd been raised in. Other than the kitchen they had entered through, there was a living area with numerous timber chairs placed around a large fireplace and a long room with beds along one wall. Ilsa counted them. There were twelve. In the castle they would have each had their own room. She thought of the spacious bedroom in the old section of the castle. Because she'd been born, they shared a single narrow room.

Guilt hit her and she hurried from the bedroom, only to face the living area. They were forced to live in three rooms and no matter how large the living room was, it couldn't compare to a castle. She sagged against the doorframe, grabbing hold. Aaron would never let her stay. She'd be forced to return to the castle and made to marry Prince Abelard. Her exhaustion returned and she closed her eyes, not knowing what to do.

"Ilsa?"

Opening her eyes, she pushed away from the doorframe at her brother's call, striding towards the kitchen. She had nearly reached it when he appeared in the doorway. "Yes?"

"They'll be home soon. Hide in the bedroom, under the far bed. You'll know when to come out. Or if you should come out."

Nodding, Ilsa returned to the bedroom, trying not to think about what was to come. She crawled under the far bed, relieved that the timber floor was as clean underneath as it was throughout the rest of the house. It wasn't long before she heard the sounds of voices and footsteps. The house was filled with laughter and talking. She listened as they spoke about their day, Benjamin admonishing them to scrape their boots outside and wash up if they wanted food.

The noise slowly reduced until

only an occasional word was spoken as they settled in the living area with their meal. Ilsa wriggled, trying to get more comfortable. When was Benjamin going to say something? Surely he didn't expect her to spend hours lying on the hard floor. Or was he going to make her stay here all night? Maybe he wasn't really going to help her. She couldn't spend an entire night lying on a hard wooden floor without even a blanket to keep her warm.

"Aaron, I was thinking that maybe we could all take turns at taking care of the house so I can help with the woodcutting," Benjamin said.

His words brought protests and arguments.

"Quiet." One voice cut into the rest.

"But Aaron-"

"Quiet," Aaron cut off the speaker again. There was a moment of silence before Aaron spoke again. "What brought this on? Fredrick didn't mean anything by his comment about the bread earlier."

"It wasn't like I-"

"Quiet, Fredrick," Aaron cut off his brother. "Well, Benjamin?"

"You've always sworn you'll kill the first woman who steps foot into our house so that none of us dare bring one home. Would you kill an innocent for what was done to us by another?" Benjamin asked.

"Who is she? Who've you met?" Fredrick asked.

"Quiet," Aaron snapped. "Get to the point, Benjamin."

"I was thinking that instead of swearing to kill the first woman who steps foot in our house you should make her take care of the house instead. Then I could be out in the woods helping all of you. Do you think I want to be stuck taking care of the house for the rest of my life?" Benjamin asked.

"He actually makes sense for once," one of them said and several agreed with him.

Ilsa could barely breathe as she waited for Aaron's answer. If he agreed then she wouldn't have to convince him of anything.

"The next woman who enters the house we'll make stay and take care of it," Aaron said.

Ilsa started to slide out from under the bed.

"Unless it's our sister," Aaron continued.

Ilsa froze.

"She I'll kill and take back my rightful place," Aaron said.

"Why would she come here?" Fredrick asked. "As if she'd want to come here when she has an entire castle to live in."

"That sounds fair," Benjamin said. "Although she'd probably prefer a quick death than to be made suffer for what she's taken from us."

Ilsa thought of the window in the middle of the wall at the foot of the beds. Could she make it there before Benjamin told them where to find her? She'd obviously been a fool to trust him.

"What do you think would be better than killing her?" Aaron asked, raising his voice above the grumbling of his brothers.

"I don't know, but letting her get away with all she's done doesn't seem right. Because of her we've been on the run for seventeen years," Benjamin said.

Ilsa eased her way to the foot of the bed, rising to a crouch, looking above the edge of the next bed and through the open doorway. Benjamin's back was to her and he faced a man with a thick, sandy brown beard that matched his hair. It was the one she'd noticed in the woods earlier. The one with the frown.

"Quiet." Aaron made a slashing motion with his hand when the rest of his brothers continued to complain. "What would you have me do with her instead?"

Benjamin shrugged. "Serve us. Have her take care of the laundry, the meals, the cleaning. Could you see a pampered princess doing the work of a servant?"

A ripple of laughter went around the room as Ilsa tried to creep closer to the window. She passed the second bed, crouching in behind the third one after checking that no one had heard her move. Her heart raced. The window was across from the sixth bed. Surely she could make it.

Aaron rose to his feet. "Not that it matters. She'll never come here. But if she ever does, she can be our servant if you want." He stretched. "I'm off to bed. It's been a long day. And tomorrow will be equally long."

Ilsa scurried to the fourth bed, her gaze darting between the open doorway and the window.

Benjamin also rose to his feet. "Strange things have been known to happen." He turned towards the bedroom as several of his brothers also rose to their feet, talking about bed.

Seeing Benjamin walk towards the bedroom, Ilsa made a dash towards the window. Benjamin broke into a run, several of his brothers demanding what he was doing.

"There's a woman in our bedroom," one of them called out.

"Grab her," another shouted.

She was halfway through the window, thinking it was possible she might manage to escape, when Benjamin reached her.

He dragged her into the bedroom. "You wanted this chance. You begged me for it. What did you think would happen? That we'd be your servants? Everyone pulls their weight around here." His words were an angry whisper.

Ilsa glared at him, wishing the light from the fireplace did more than cast his face into shadows. "You want to punish me."

Aaron pulled Ilsa from Benjamin's grip. "Who is this?"

"Our sister," Benjamin said.

Ilsa struggled to pull away from Aaron. His grip tightened and fear exploded through her. "Please. Let me go. I didn't know. Please."

"All that was about saving her?" Aaron demanded.

Benjamin shook his head. "No. It was to see if she's worth saving." He stepped between Ilsa and Aaron. "Let her go. You said she could be our servant if I want."

Ilsa quit struggling, a glimmer of hope forming.

Aaron's grip remained tight as he stared at Benjamin. "She's your responsibility. If she escapes, you pay the price."

"Done." Benjamin nodded and grabbed hold of Ilsa's arm when Aaron let it go and strode towards his bed. Benjamin faced her. "Are you going to run?"

"Will you trust me if I say no?"

It took Benjamin a minute to answer. "Probably not." He sighed. "What am I meant to do with you?"

She had no answers for him. Only questions and she didn't think now was the time to ask them. "I won't run. I have nothing to run to." Surely she could prove to her brothers that none of this was her fault. She just needed a chance.

Benjamin led her to the living room, still gripping her arm. "You can sleep in front of the fire. We have a couple of spare blankets you can use." He stared at her for several minutes.

Ilsa met his steady gaze, wondering what he wanted. Did he wish to tell her something or was he waiting for her to speak? She had no idea and thought it best to remain silent. Around them the living room was empty, all their brothers having retreated to the bedroom.

Letting go of her arm, Benjamin spun abruptly, striding back to the bedroom. He returned with the blankets he'd mentioned, holding them out to her.

"Thank you."

"If you run, I will track you down and I will give you to Aaron to deal with."

"I won't run." She watched as Benjamin walked away, leaving her alone in front of the fireplace. Not knowing what else to do, she wrapped the blankets around herself and curled up in front of the fire wishing she'd been offered food.

It took ages for her to fall asleep on the hard floor. Missing her own bed, she finally drifted off to sleep to be woken by the sound of voices and footsteps. Struggling to untangle herself from her blankets, Ilsa saw her brothers leave their bedroom singularly and in pairs. Some of them yawned, some stumbled and some talked quietly. Rubbing her eyes, she covered her own yawn with a hand before she stumbled to her feet and began to fold up the blankets she'd used. Placing them to one side, out of the way, she hurried after Benjamin who entered the kitchen.

It was time to start proving her innocence. Time to earn her place. "Can I help?"

Benjamin handed her a pot. "Fill

this with water and put it on to boil while I light the stove."

They worked quietly together. The only conversation was orders from Benjamin as they made tea and porridge. While they waited for it to cook, they mixed bread dough and set it aside to rise. By the time their eleven brothers had left and the kitchen was tidy and vegetables prepared for the midday meal of stew, Ilsa had begun to wonder what had possessed her to run away from home. She brought to mind an image of Prince Abelard and his constant harping about what he expected of her.

Straightening her shoulders, she turned to Benjamin. "What needs to be done now?"

"Make the beds while I bake apple pies for tonight."

With her shoulders still straight, Ilsa strode to the bedroom, her gaze pausing at each bed. Twelve of them. What had her parents been thinking having so many children? She guessed this wasn't getting the beds made. Walking slowly, she crossed the room and started with the bed she'd hidden under the previous night.

The next couple of weeks passed in a similar fashion. Ilsa cooked and cleaned with Benjamin, learning how to make all the different foods they ate. Several of her earlier attempts were charred, but it didn't take her long to learn with Benjamin watching over her and pointing out all her mistakes.

When Benjamin took the midday meal to their brothers, he made her stay behind and when everyone returned in the evening, no one talked to her. Aaron even went so far as to tell her 'quiet' whenever she tried to talk to any of them. Each day she learned something new. To shoot a bow and hunt for deer, to catch fish in the nearby stream and to tend the vegetable garden at the side of the house near the stable. And every day she tried to get her brothers to talk to her. Only Benjamin did, but only to give her orders or instructions.

One evening, Ilsa helped Benjamin serve the fried fish they'd caught that afternoon and wished she could join in the conversations around her. She watched as Aaron had a bite of his fish and turned to Benjamin with a nod.

"Perfect."

Benjamin looked towards Ilsa, but said nothing.

Anger, loneliness and frustration

arrowed through her. "I caught it and I cooked it."

Aaron frowned in her direction before he turned back to Benjamin. "Be careful in the woods. We saw a bear today. She had two cubs and they all looked scrawny."

She was tempted to throw the food at Aaron. Instead, she quietly took a deep breath and slowly released it as she glared at him.

Benjamin served the next brother in line. "I'll carry the bow when I bring your food tomorrow."

Aaron nodded before he left the kitchen to take his place in his seat by the fire.

Ilsa served one of her brothers as she watched Aaron leave. She was beginning to think he'd never forgive her. That nothing she did would make a difference. Once she'd served the last one in line, she filled her own bowl and joined them in the living area. There was no chair for her and like all the other nights, she sat in the corner, her back against the wall as she stared into the flames, wishing she was a part of the conversations.

Maybe she should leave. But she couldn't run. Benjamin had said he'd hunt her down and she believed his words. What would it take to convince him she'd made a mistake? And where could she go? Not back to the castle. That left nowhere for her to go. Finishing her meal, she rose and quietly gathered the empty bowls, taking them to the kitchen to wash.

As soon as the kitchen was clean and tidy, Ilsa gathered her blankets and spread them in front of the fire. About to lie down, she noticed a shape in the bedroom doorway. It was Aaron. He stared at her and she remained standing, staring back at him. Finally he turned without a word and made his way to his bed, the one closest to the door.

Ilsa continued to stare after him for several more minutes before she lay down. It felt like she'd barely gotten to sleep before the noise of her brothers rising woke her. The morning passed quickly and soon she had the house to herself while she waited for Benjamin to return from delivering the food to their brothers. She felt no less alone being by herself than she felt surrounded by her brothers. Feeling restless and having finished her chores, she wandered through the rooms trying to decide what to do. In the kitchen, her gaze fell on the bow and she remembered

Aaron's warning from the night before.

Surely Benjamin would be fine. Maybe Aaron was only being overly cautious. He did take his responsibility to his brothers very seriously. But what if the bear was still around? Would Benjamin be safe? Bears tended to avoid people whenever possible, why would this one be any different?

No matter what she told herself, Ilsa couldn't stop thinking about the bear until she finally gathered up the bow and a quiverful of arrows and headed down the well-worn path leading into the forest. Twigs snapped underfoot and leaves crunched. The sounds seemed to fill the air around her. Benjamin probably wasn't going to be happy about her wandering around the forest. Each day he asked her if she was going to run away. Each day she said no. Taking off with his bow didn't look good.

A sound ahead had her freezing on the path. What had that been? It was quiet again. She hurried forward, the bow in one hand, an arrow in the other. There was a roar and someone cursing and Ilsa realised it was Benjamin. She ran along the path, her heart beating rapidly. Rounding a bend in the path, she came to a halt as she saw Benjamin up a tree, holding a hunting knife. The bear was at the foot of the tree, trying to reach him, roaring each time he struck out at her. The cubs Aaron had mentioned were nowhere in sight.

Benjamin raised his head to stare at her. "Ilsa! Run!"

The bear took the opportunity to

climb up the tree a few inches, roaring when Benjamin struck at her again.

"Not Benjamin," she whispered. Not the only brother who was willing to give her a chance. With trembling hands, Ilsa lifted the bow, drawing back the arrow. She could do this. Hadn't she helped Benjamin bring down a deer recently? Letting go of the string, she watched as the arrow flew towards the bear, taking another arrow from the quiver.

"Run!"

The arrow struck the bear's paw and with a louder roar, she faced Ilsa, loping towards her. Ilsa let go another arrow, her heart in her throat. It flew too wide. Walking backwards, Ilsa fired a third arrow. The bear rose on hind legs as the arrow hit.

"Run, Ilsa. Run!" Benjamin scrambled down from the tree.

The arrow hit the bear, then she was on Ilsa. All she could see was the open mouth coming for her with large white teeth that looked needle sharp. Saliva and blood dripped onto her. Ilsa screamed and struggled to get out from under the bear as pain exploded in her shoulder.

Benjamin appeared above the bear, sinking his hunting knife into it. The bear roared, turning on him, striking out at Benjamin as he withdrew the knife and sunk it in once more, this time into the chest.

The bear fell backwards, half on Ilsa and she tried to push the weight off herself. Then there were hands helping from every direction, voices demanding what was happening. Ilsa realised she was sobbing and tried to stop. Aaron's face was in hers and she tried to make sense of his demands, only able to shake her head. Finally sounds began to make understandable words again.

"I forgot to take the bow," Benjamin said. "She saved my life."

Ilsa shook her head again. "I only made her angry. Benjamin killed her."

"Why?" Aaron continued to stare at her.

She had no idea what he wanted to know.

"Well?" Aaron demanded.

She shrank back from the anger in his voice. "I don't know what you're asking me."

"Why were you in the woods? Why did you have the bow and why did you attack the bear instead of running like any sane person would have?"

"You told Benjamin to take the bow. I found it in the kitchen so I was taking it to him." She swallowed, trying not to think of the snarling mouth with dagger sharp teeth that had filled her vision minutes before. "I didn't think the bear would be that hard to kill. The deer was easy."

Benjamin pushed Aaron out of the way. "Let me take her home. She's bleeding. Look at her shoulder."

Ilsa looked at her shoulder and saw the claw marks, which oozed blood, slicing through the sleeve of her dress. Her stomach lurched and the pain she felt in her shoulder now made sense.

"Come on." Benjamin held out a hand.

Using her uninjured arm, Ilsa took his hand, her legs unsteady. One of her brothers handed Benjamin the bow she'd dropped and another gave him the pot. Aaron ordered Fredrick to go with them.

Back in the kitchen of the house, Benjamin seated her in a chair that Fredrick brought from the living room. He started to clean her wound.

Fredrick paced the kitchen several times before he turned to them. "I'll get back to work." He hurried out the door with a glance over his shoulder.

Ilsa drew in her breath sharply as Benjamin dabbed at her wound again with a cloth.

"Sorry." Once he'd cleaned the wound and dressed it, he stared at her. "Thank you. The branch I was clinging to wasn't going to hold my weight much longer."

Her trembling increased. Words were beyond her.

"Why didn't you run?"

She lowered her gaze, her voice barely a whisper. "I didn't want you to die." She met his gaze. "You're the only one who's given me a chance."

He crushed her to him. "I'm sorry. I'm really sorry. I never believed you. I thought it would all turn out to be a trick. I kept waiting for you to betray us. To wake one night with an assassin about to cut my throat."

Ilsa felt her tears dampen Benjamin's shirt. "I never knew about any of you. They never told me. No one did."

* * *

Things changed. Her brothers spoke to her. One morning Fredrick offered her some of his precious honey, that he shared with no one, for her porridge. Another morning she started to sit in her usual place on the floor against the wall only to notice there was an empty chair. She counted her brothers, finding all twelve were seated.

Her shoulder was as good as healed when she came back from fishing one afternoon to make the beds Benjamin had said she could do after she'd caught dinner, only to find there was a thirteenth bed that had linen sitting folded on its mattress.

They also asked her questions. About her life, their parents and the boring Prince Abelard that Isaac, her second oldest brother, offered to kill for her. She shook her head, thanking him, and saying he wasn't worth starting a war over.

After several months had passed, Benjamin started helping their brothers work and left Ilsa to take care of the house, only staying home when she planned to go hunting. The house was quiet without them and she looked forward to taking them their midday meal and hearing their noisy camaraderie. Returning from feeding them one day, she found an old woman sobbing on the doorstep.

Running forward, Ilsa dropped the pot by the door, putting an arm around the woman. "What's wrong? Can I help you with something?"

"You cannot imagine how grateful I am to find someone. I stopped to water my horse at a stream not far from here and wolves attacked me. They killed my horse while I ran. You must help me get home."

Ilsa's gaze searched the area, listening for the wolves that had attacked the woman. "Where are they now?"

"Probably still feasting upon my horse. Please, can you help me get home?"

Ilsa shook her head. "No, but my brothers could take you home when they return this evening. Where are you from?" When the woman told her, Ilsa decided that even her brothers wouldn't leave so late in the day to travel that distance. It would be long past dark before they arrived. "Why don't you come in and I'll make you a cup of tea and something to eat? You can stay the night and someone can take you home in the morning."

"No, no. I couldn't do that. My widowed daughter is due to have her first child any day now. I don't want to worry her. I noticed your horse out the back, surely you could take me home and be back before dark."

Ilsa nearly said yes, but worried what her brothers would think if they returned to find her gone. She didn't want to risk losing their trust after how long it had taken her to gain it. But the thought of the old woman's poor daughter worrying about her mother and not knowing what had happened to her weighed heavy on her mind. "I'll lend you my horse. Return it when you can. Just let me saddle her for you."

"Are you sure you cannot travel with me? I would feel much safer with a companion."

"I'm sorry. My brothers would worry if I wasn't here when they arrived home." Ilsa finally convinced the old woman that she couldn't travel with her and went to saddle the horse. She stood waving to the old woman as she rode away, hoping she'd done the right thing and her horse would be returned.

That evening, it was Fredrick who noticed her horse was missing and she told her brothers what had happened.

"Are you crazy?" Isaac demanded. "You'll never see your horse again."

"She must be," Fredrick said. "Why else would she choose to live with us?"

The living room was filled with laughter and Ilsa joined in. "She'll return it. She promised me." She tried to sound more positive than she felt.

"If she doesn't, I'll go to the village and ask after her," Aaron said.

Ilsa stared at her oldest brother, surprised he'd go to so much trouble for her when he'd been the one who'd caused her the most grief. "Thank you."

"I'm not about to let anyone take

advantage of my family. Now eat your food before it's cold."

She ducked her head before he noticed her smile and continued eating her meal.

Ilsa was relieved when two days later the old woman rode up on a horse, leading the mare. Going out to greet the old woman, she helped her dismount, taking the reins of her horse.

The old woman held out a small folded up piece of parchment. "For you. To thank you for your help."

Ilsa took the gift feeling bumps inside the parchment. "What is it?"

"Seeds." The old woman gestured towards the house. "To grow flowers to brighten your home."

"Thank you." Ilsa smiled. "Would you like to come in and have a cup of tea? I've just finished baking apple pies."

The old woman shook her head. "No, I must be on my way. I do not want to leave my daughter alone too long. She still hasn't had the child and I wish to be there when she does."

"Of course." Ilsa helped the woman mount her horse and watched as she rode away. When she was alone again, she looked at the seeds. There were twelve of them. She smiled at the irony. A flower for each of her brothers. She didn't think they'd appreciate the thought.

Planting them across the front of the house, she watered the area before she returned to her chores. It was Isaac who, that evening, asked why the ground was all scratched up at the front of the house. Ilsa told them about the old woman returning her horse and giving her the seeds in thanks.

Aaron nodded. "Good. That saves me a trip into town."

The conversation then turned to how long it had been since any of them had gone to town and Fredrick tried to convince his oldest brother it was long past time they went. Ilsa listened to them, occasionally joining the conversation when her opinion was sought. It was far different living with her brothers than it had been living in a castle. The place might be smaller, but here her thoughts and feelings mattered. Here she could be herself instead of what the people needed.

* * *

Over the next two months, Ilsa tended her garden, watching as the plants grew. Isaac grumbled about what a waste of time it was, but one morning she found him edging her garden in rocks. When she thanked him he grumbled that it made the place look messy without some kind of border. Hiding a smile, Ilsa returned inside to serve their morning meal.

The day the flowers finally bloomed, Ilsa stood admiring them in the late afternoon sunshine. Each one was perfect. Hearing her brothers coming closer, she decided to pick them and put them in the kitchen so they would be the first things they saw when they came home from work. Stepping inside, she grabbed a knife from the kitchen and hurried out again. She could see her brothers starting to emerge from the forest. She would have to hurry if she wanted to put the flowers in the kitchen before they came inside. Facing the flowers again, she cut each one off, leaving a long stem. Surprised not to already hear her brothers' usual talking and joking, she looked over her shoulder to see how close they were.

She couldn't see them, only ravens. She spun, taking a step forward, the flowers clutched in one hand, the knife in the other. The ravens squawked and squabbled with each other, one of them flying to her and landing at her feet.

Where were her brothers? "Benjamin! Aaron!" No one answered, but another raven flew to her and landed at her feet. She took a step backwards. "Fredrick! Isaac!" Another two birds joined the ones at her feet. Ilsa stared down at them. She slowly turned, her gaze searching the area. Where were they? She called each of her brothers' names and one by one the ravens flew to her. The flowers tumbled to the ground, the knife joining them. "No!" She backed away until the house prevented further retreat. "No!" She shook her head.

Laughter came from the forest and the old woman rode out on her horse. "Did you think you could escape your father forever?"

Ilsa pointed an accusing finger at the old woman. "You! You did this. Why?"

"Your father's men will be here soon to take you home and hunt down the ravens."

"No." She waved her hands. "Fly. Go. Quickly. Before they get here. Don't let them kill you." She brushed the back of her hand across her cheeks, trying to wipe away the tears, but they continued to fall. Grabbing the knife, she ran forward, dragging the old woman from her horse before she could ride away. "Tell me how to break the spell. Tell me." She held the knife at the old woman's throat, surprised at the anger that rushed through her. Surprised it took so much effort not to kill her.

"You will never manage."

"Tell me." She pressed the knife harder, seeing a line of blood trickle down the old woman's throat.

"Once the sun sets on this day you cannot speak another sound for seven years. Not a word, no laughter, nothing. One sound from your lips and your brothers will instantly die. If you manage, your brothers will again be themselves when the sun sets on the last day of those seven years.”

“You promise me this? You swear it on your life?”

“Yes.”

She remembered lending the woman her horse so she could return home. “Do you have a pregnant daughter?”

“No.” The woman laughed, pushing at her hand that held the knife.

Ilsa shoved the old woman away from her, angry words wanting to pour from her. But she didn’t have time. In the distance she heard the sound of hounds. She had to escape. Looking into the sky, she saw the sun wasn’t far off setting. Running inside, she grabbed the bow and quiver full of arrows, some food, and the bag she’d arrived with before running to the stable to saddle her horse. Looking around, she saw no sign of the old woman. Recalling the day she'd left home, she mounted her horse and galloped towards the stream. Above her flew one of the ravens. She didn't have a clue which of her brothers it was.

Plunging into the stream, she rode her horse through the water, staying in it for hours to throw the hounds off the scent. It was dawn when she finally left the stream and looked for somewhere to rest awhile.

Her days soon fell into a pattern. She hunted and gathered what food she could, avoiding villages and people. There was nearly always a raven with her, mostly the smallest one that she was beginning to think was Benjamin. Occasionally it was a large, angry looking raven that she believed to be Aaron. They would watch over her at night and wake her if there was any danger.

Breaking into a house several weeks after her brothers had become ravens, she stole some parchment, worried she'd lose track of the days. Then each day as the sun set, she pulled the parchment from her bag and marked off another day with a piece of charcoal she'd kept from one of her campfires.

Months passed and winter arrived. She was forced to set her horse free, unable to find feed for her. She stole blankets from a house, leaving several of the coins she'd taken with her when she'd first left home. Then it was spring again and bending forward to drink from a melted pool of water, she stared at the reflection of the wild girl who looked back at her.   Tears streamed down her face and Benjamin landed on her shoulder and gently pecked at her cheek. Words filled her throat and she ached to speak them.

Setting Benjamin on the ground, she leaned forward and dunked her head in the water, washing away the tears and dirt that streaked her face. She had to be stronger than this. It wasn't even a year and yet already she was wallowing in self-pity and desperate to talk. Her brothers deserved better from her than that. Drying her face on the cleanest part of her dress, she sat at the pool, finger combing her hair. It took her hours to remove the knots and twigs. When she rose from the ground, it was late afternoon and in the distance she heard the sound of hounds.

Fear struck and she turned to run

into the forest. A man on a horse came out of the trees, a smile on his face. She raced off to her right, heading for the forest. Before she reached the trees, she was scooped off her feet and deposited on the horse in front of the man. Struggling to escape didn't help. He only drew her closer.

"You're safe. I won't hurt you. Stop trying to get away."

She stilled, turning her head to look into his blue eyes. He had light brown hair and continued to smile at her, his expression kind and sincere. She thought of the old woman who had seemed honest, but look what trouble she had brought. Her brothers had been turned into ravens.

"What is your name?"

Ilsa shook her head.

"You won't tell me your name?"

He laughed softly. "Or is it that you don't have a name?"

She could only shake her head again.

"Then how about I start the introductions? I'm Edric. Now what is your name?"

She stared up at him, wanting to escape. Desperate to escape before she accidentally made a sound. Any sound.

Edric sighed. "I should probably return to my party before they come looking for me."

Ilsa tried to slide off the horse, but his arms tightened around her.

"I can't leave you in the forest on your own. It isn't safe. You can come home with me. My mother will make you welcome."

She wished she could argue with him and tell him exactly how long she'd survived alone in the forest without help. Instead, she could only shake her head and point towards her bag left at the water's edge. She couldn't leave it behind. How else would she know the amount of time that had passed? It took her several minutes, but she finally got Edric to ride closer and he saw her bag. He dismounted and grabbed it and her bow and quiver before he swung up behind her again. He dragged her back into place before him and she glared at him for preventing her attempt at escaping.

"Your Highness, we've been looking for you for ages."

Edric rode towards the man who had ridden out of the forest. "And now you've found me. Did you manage to catch the buck we were chasing, Gregor?"

Gregor looked towards Ilsa with a grin. "Yes, but it isn't as interesting a catch as the wench you've caught."

"Mind your manners, Gregor. Watch how you address the lady."

"Of course, Your Highness." He bowed at the waist, his horse shifting restlessly beneath him.

"Allow me to introduce you to one of my nobles, Lord Gregor. He is usually much better mannered than that," Edric said.

Ilsa stared at Gregor, aware of the man at her back who prevented her from running. Gregor was dark haired, dark eyed and had a smile that showed no resentment at the rebuke from his king. How was it that after all the months of hiding she'd fallen into the hands of a king? Had she no good luck left at all?

"It is a pleasure to meet you, my

lady." Gregor once again bowed, this time not as low.

Ilsa inclined her head, knowing that he deserved some type of reply.

Gregor laughed. "It seems like she has been rendered speechless by your illustrious presence, Your Highness."

Before Edric could reply, a group of riders burst from the trees, a buck tied to the back of a riderless horse. Questions and comments were spoken all at once and ignoring them, Edric rode on, calling over his shoulder, "Time to go home."

The entire journey, Ilsa looked for an opportunity to escape. There was none and she soon found herself in the courtyard of a castle, being helped from Edric's horse. Orders were given that she was to be taken care of and servants rushed her away and bathed and dressed her. She was then led to Edric who was seated at a small table with only two chairs. On the table was a tea service and a tray of small cakes.

Edric rose as she entered the room and gestured towards the other seat. "You look lovely. Would you like to join me for tea?"

Ilsa curtseyed before she allowed Edric to seat her at the table, smiling her thanks.

Edric stared down at her for a moment. "What were you doing in the forest? You're obviously a lady."

Ilsa's smile faded and she could only stare up at Edric. It wasn't the first time that she wished she could read and write, but her father had believed it was only for priests and scribes. She was relieved when Edric sighed and sat across from her.

Gesturing towards the teapot,

Edric asked, "Would you like to pour?"

Ilsa nodded and poured the tea, offering the tray of cakes to him. He stared at her a moment before he took one. A call came from a window, a gentle squawk that drew Ilsa's attention. Benjamin sat on the ledge, turning his head from side to side.

Edric stood, hurrying towards the window, waving his hands. "Go, go on, go away."

Ilsa rushed after him, grabbing his hands and shaking her head. Her eyes pleaded with him to leave her brother alone.

"This is your bird?"

She nodded, then shook her head, then nodded again. How was she to explain that he wasn't hers, but her brother? She kept hold of Edric's hands.

Edric tugged one of his hands from her grasp, running a knuckle across her cheek. "Can you talk at all?"

She shook her head.

"Do you have a name?"

A nod.

"Then I will just have to guess it."

She smiled up at him, letting go of his hand.

"Is it Jana? Ursula? Theda?"

She continued to shake her head as he rattled off names.

Finally he led her back to the table. "This has probably cooled by now. Let me call for fresh tea."

Ilsa shook her head, taking a sip of her tea. It didn't matter to her if it was cold or warm. It had been months since she'd enjoyed a cup of tea that any temperature suited her. Sitting quietly, Benjamin still on the window ledge, Ilsa listened as Edric spoke, occasionally nodding or shaking her head, a couple of times shrugging.

The tea had long since been drunk and the cakes eaten when a regal woman, dressed in black, strode into the room. "There you are, Edric. No one seemed to know where you were."

Edric rose to his feet. "Mother, I would like you to meet the young lady I rescued today." He turned to Ilsa. This is my mother, the Dowager Queen Sofia."

Ilsa rose to her feet, curtseying deeply to the woman who stared down her nose at her. The dowager queen wore numerous jewels, including a large green emerald necklace that matched her eyes. There were smaller emeralds threaded through her dark blond hair, which was piled atop her head in an elaborate style.

Sofia barely gave Ilsa a nod. "You aren't even ready. Several kings and queens have arrived, along with their daughters. Being the last one in to dinner would be insulting."

"I'll be there in time, now if you would excuse me, I'll escort my lady to her room first." Edric held out his arm.

Ilsa gratefully took his arm and let him show her to her room, glad to escape the glare Sofia gave her. Obviously his mother wasn't going to make her welcome like Edric believed.

In her room, Ilsa leaned against the window ledge, staring outside at the star studded night. Turning away, she took the parchment from her bag that was sitting on a chest at the foot of her bed and marked off another day. Closing her eyes, she tried not to think of how much time there was still to go before her brothers would be free of the spell. A grumbling squawk drew her attention and she opened her eyes to see Aaron sitting on her window ledge. She wanted to reassure him that she wouldn't speak. That one day they'd be themselves again. Putting the parchment back in her bag, noticing the rest of her things were untouched and the bow and quiver were with it on the chest, she strode to the window. Staring down at Aaron, she pressed her fingers to her lips and willed him to understand. With a nod of his head and another growl like squawk, he flew off.

* * *

Days passed and every morning she joined Edric for the morning meal where he would offer more names. Sometimes she smiled at the names he offered, but each time she shook her head. It was one year, three months and five days since her brothers had been turned into ravens when Edric walked with her in the gardens.

He asked her name after name until finally he asked, "Ilka?"

She grabbed at his shirt, shaking her head.

Edric frowned. "Was that your name?"

She nodded, then shook her head again, still holding onto his shirt.

"I'm close?"

She nodded, grinning.

Edric laughed, grabbing her

around the waist and spinning her. "I'm close!"

Laughter threatened to escape and she bit her lip to hold it back, pushing away from him.

He let her go and stared down at her. "How close? Very?"

A nod.

"The beginning?"

Another nod.

"The middle?"

This time she shook her head.

"The end?"

Another nod.

Edric grinned. "I will figure it out. Not right now though. My mother promised I'd take the daughter of one of our neighbours riding." He sighed. "I would much prefer if she didn't try and arrange my days." He raised Ilsa's hand to his lips and kissed it, staring at her a moment longer before he strode away.

Ilsa watched him leave, wishing she could tell him her name. A cry drew her attention and she saw Benjamin in a nearby tree. She held up her hand and he flew down and landed on it, nuzzling her cheek. Words clawed at her throat again and she forced them away. She could do this. She had to. Benjamin flew off and she headed back to her room. It was better to stay in her room. No one expected anything of her in there.

It took Edric another day before he said, "Ilsa."

Grinning, she threw her arms around him, relieved at hearing her name after so long. Edric laughed, drawing her close, his lips meeting hers. Her first reaction was shock, but that was soon replaced by joy.

When he drew away from her, he said, "Come riding with me today. My mother will have to learn not to organise my days for me. She can make apologies to the princess she invited on my behalf."

Ilsa stared up at him, wanting to say yes, but Sofia already hated her enough without making it worse. She slowly shook her head, drawing away from him. Even when he continued to try and convince her, she still shook her head. Eventually he gave up and they finished their walk through the gardens in companionable silence.

When Edric left, Aaron flew down to her shoulder, scolding her. She nodded her head, but still he continued. Eventually she pushed him away and he rose into the air, still berating her. Benjamin swooped past him, and Aaron chased after his brother with one last squawk for Ilsa. She stared after them, wishing she hadn't been so stupid as to trust the old woman. But how could she have known her father would send a witch after her?

Days passed and every day Edric spent hours with Ilsa. He finally convinced her to go riding with him, join him at the elaborate dinners held every evening and to attend the balls his mother arranged.

It was exactly two years since her brothers had been turned into ravens when Edric seated her in a rose arbour, kneeling at her feet. "Ilsa–"

She shook her head vehemently, rising to her feet, trying to draw him up. As much as she wanted to hear what he was likely to say, she couldn't let him. It wouldn't be fair to chain him to someone trying to break a curse.

Edric rose, pulling her close to him. "Ilsa, please listen. I want you to be my wife. All the princesses my mother keeps inviting here are boring creatures. Every moment I spend with them I'm thinking of how quickly I can leave them and return to you."

She shook her head, pressing her fingers to her lips.

Edric drew her fingers away. "I don't care that you can't speak. I still manage to figure out what you want to say. I'm sure I'll get better at it the longer we're together. Please, Ilsa. Please say you'll be my bride."

She continued to shake her head, saying no each time he asked her over the next couple of months. In the end, his persistence paid off and she nodded, sliding her arms around his waist, resting her head on his shoulder and ignoring Aaron who scolded her from a nearby tree.

"What a terrible noise that raven's making," Edric said. "I'll let the hunters know so they can get rid of him."

Ilsa drew away from him, running towards Aaron, holding out a hand for him, beckoning him forward. He flew to her shoulder, pecking her sharply on the cheek. Edric reached her side and tried to come close, but she held him back with a hand. Her shoulder, with Aaron on it, was turned away from him.

"If they mean that much to you, I'll tell the hunters to never kill another raven again. Will that please you?"

She relaxed her hand and let him come close, nodding her head.

Edric smiled. "I thought it was only one of them you were fond of. Now it seems it's all ravens."

Ilsa answered his smile with one of her own, ignoring Aaron's soft grumbling.

"Let's go and tell my mother the happy news."

Ilsa pointed to the raven.

Edric laughed. "All right. First I'll tell the hunters that no ravens are to ever be harmed. Then we tell my mother."

Ilsa nodded, although she dreaded Sofia's reaction when she heard the news. She was right to dread the reaction. Sofia was frosty, telling them not to be so hasty, finally managing to convince them to at least have a long engagement.

The engagement that originally was meant to last a year dragged on.

The end of that year brought with it a terrible fire in the village that Sofia said would make them appear callous if they went ahead and celebrated while their own people were having problems. Before the year after could draw to a close, a mysterious illness struck down many of the villagers.

Four years eight months and twelve days after Ilsa's brothers had been turned into ravens, Edric lost patience and said that they'd be married within a month regardless of what else happened. Even if they had to do it barefoot, penniless and with the castle and village in rubble around their feet.

Ilsa agreed and four years, nine months and seven days from when her brothers had become ravens Ilsa nodded instead of saying 'I do' and became Queen Ilsa. There was one moment where she thought she might break into noisy sobs when all twelve of her brothers flew into the church and came to roost on statues, window ledges and even a pew. Fredrick was the one on the pew, but Aaron flew down and landed on her shoulder.

A noblewoman, sitting on the pew Fredrick had landed on, screamed. "Demons! We're being invaded by demons."

A ripple of laughter went through some of the crowd, but others muttered in agreement. Ilsa, worried for her brother, held out her hand and he flew to her. She glared at Fredrick for a moment before she pointed to a window ledge where Benjamin perched. When Fredrick had flown away, she turned back to Edric who was smiling down at her.

"See, even the birds can understand you. How can I fail to understand you when such simple creatures can?" He took her hands, holding onto them throughout the rest of the ceremony.

Life settled into a routine and as the years slowly passed Ilsa began to think she would manage to remain silent for the seven years. There were only three months left when rumours began to circulate and the priest started to preach about demons appearing in the guise of animals that acted oddly. People started to whisper about how their queen spoke to ravens that understood her and question why she had remained barren after years of marriage.

Another week passed before Edric spoke to her about her inability to make sounds. "Why do you never laugh?"

Ilsa tilted her head at an angle, to let him know she didn't understand what he was asking.

"My mother had a little girl with her today who couldn't speak. Not a single word. But she could laugh." He waited a moment as if Ilsa would finally be able to answer him. "Why can't you laugh?"

Ilsa shook her head, reaching for his hands and squeezing them lightly. She wished she could laugh. She wished she could speak. Even for Edric she wouldn't. Not until her brothers were human again.

A couple of weeks later, Edric asked her, "Must you let the ravens into the castle? Our people are worried. They fear they're demons."

Ilsa shook her head, grabbing his hands and holding on tightly.

"The priest says evil creatures can bring evil into a home."

Again she shook her head, narrowing her eyes. She wouldn't let him get rid of her brothers.

"They don't have to kill them, just chase them away."

Ilsa pulled away from him, tears forming in her eyes as she backed away from Edric.

He came forward reaching for her. "It was only a thought. Please, don't cry. I won't let anyone chase them away."

More weeks passed until there were only two weeks left until Ilsa's brothers would be human again. She spent hours watching the sun cross the sky, impatiently waiting for time to pass. She was sitting by a window watching the shadows lengthen when Edric found her.

"I've been searching for you for hours."

She looked up at him, tilting her head to the side in question.

"All the nobles have left and so have most of the servants. Surely now you can see the ravens have to go. Ilsa, our people are terrified of them."

She shook her head.

"Ilsa, be sensible. They're worried they're demons."

Again she shook her head. It wouldn't be long before they would understand. Fourteen days. If she could only convince him to wait a little longer.

"Ilsa–"

She rose to her feet and pressed her fingers to his lips and again shook her head.

Edric sighed. "What will we do for servants? We don't even have anyone to cook our meals."

Ilsa smiled and headed for the kitchen.

Edric walked beside her. "Where are you going?" He walked silently beside her, stopping at the kitchen doorway and watching Ilsa pull out pots, pans and food. "Do you know what you're doing?"

Ilsa paused in her work and nodded, a smile forming. She waited for Edric to nod and turn away before she returned to her work. The kitchen might be larger than the one in her brothers' home, but she would be able to use it as easily.

When there was only a week left, Edric marched into the kitchen. "They have to go. We haven't a single soldier left. Anyone could invade and there'd be no one to stop them."

Ilsa removed the bread from the oven, placing the pan on the wooden table. She pointed first to Edric and then to herself.

"We're only two people. What could we do against an army?"

Ilsa mimed drawing back a bow and loosing an arrow.

"Be sensible."

She placed her hands on her hips and glared at Edric. If he only knew, then he'd realise she was being sensible.

"Are you trying to ruin us?"

She shook her head, dropping her hands to her side. She remembered the words her mother had spoken to her years ago. 'One day you will have to make the same hard choices.' She wasn't about to make the same choice her parents had made. She wouldn't sacrifice her brothers for her country.

"Then why won't you let me get rid of the ravens?"

She pressed a hand to her heart.

"I do love you."

She shook her head, wishing she could find a way to tell him she loved the ravens as much as she loved him. That it would be impossible for her to choose between them.

Edric crossed the room, wrapping his arms around her. "I do love you, Ilsa."

She rested her head on his shoulder. Only seven more days. Not long and she'd be able to tell him everything.

On the evening of the second last day, Sofia marched into the kitchen, Gregor beside her and Edric following. Dusting the flour from her hands, Ilsa looked to each of them.

"Mother, I won't allow it," Edric said.

"You would ruin us all for a serving wench? Look at her." Sofia pointed towards Ilsa. "This is where she belongs for all her airs and graces. What noblewoman can cook as well as she can?"

"You're wrong," Edric said.

"She's beautiful, but can't you see what she's doing to you, Edric?" Gregor asked. "Anyone would think you were under a spell. Look around you? Where are your people? There is only your mother and I and we can see clearly even if you can't."

Ilsa eyed the doorway behind them. Would she be able to make it without them stopping her?

"Where were you weeks ago? You left when the rest of the nobles did," Edric said to Gregor.

"I had things to attend to at home, but I'm back now and shocked at how you've let things go. She must be a witch. Nothing else explains it," Gregor said.

Ilsa took cautious steps to the side, working her way around the table.

"Burn her at the stake and break her hold on you," Sofia said. "I know you believe you love her, but you aren't thinking clearly. If you were, you wouldn't have let things go so far. Think, Edric."

"No. She can't be a witch." Edric slowly shook his head. "She can't."

"She speaks not a sound, not even to laugh," Sofia said.

"That doesn't mean anything. She isn't a witch." Edric crossed the room, taking one of Ilsa's hands. "Tell me you're not a witch."

Ilsa shook her head, reaching up to

place her palm against his cheek. Two days. Couldn't they have waited two days?

"Of course she would say no. Who is going to admit to being a witch? Kill her familiars and maybe that will break the spell," Sofia said.

Ilsa shook her head, pulling away from Edric. She tried to run from the kitchen, but Gregor grabbed her around the waist. Struggling to get free, Ilsa heard Edric shouting at Gregor to let her go. Sofia demanded that Gregor hold on.

"Tie her to the stake. Let her familiars come and try and save her and then kill them. That should be enough to break the spell and you'll see for yourself that she's a witch," Sofia said.

"I couldn't do that to her," Edric said.

Tears slid silently down Ilsa's cheeks as she stopped struggling, unable to escape the arms holding her. She wanted to beg Edric to help her, but she forced the words down, pleading only with her eyes.

It didn't help. Hours later, after Sofia and Gregor finally convinced him, Edric watched as Ilsa was led from the kitchen and tied at the stake that had been set up in the courtyard.

When two servants began to pile logs up around her feet, Edric called out to them, "No. I won't have you do that. It's more than enough that she's been tied up."

"It must look like we mean to burn her," Sofia said. "How else will we convince her familiars to come close enough so you and Gregor can shoot them from the sky?"

The sun was rising when Edric let

the servants start piling logs up around Ilsa's feet. Once they'd finished, he came forward, resting his palm against her cheek. "I don't want to believe them. I really don't, but I can think of no other way to prove them wrong. I know you're fond of those birds, but I can't let a handful of birds ruin our kingdom."

Ilsa turned away from him, tears streaming silently down her face.

Edric let his hand fall to his side. "I hope one day you'll forgive me, but I can't let our kingdom fall into ruin for a dozen ravens. I'm sorry, but I can't."

Hours passed and then it was the middle of the day and Edric was bringing her water and putting the cup to her lips. Sofia berated him, complaining the familiars would never be fooled into coming close.

As the sun dropped lower, Sofia turned to the two servants. "Light it."

"No," Edric shouted.

"Now."

The servants scurried towards Ilsa at Sofia's command.

"Don't you dare." Edric started forward, but Gregor grabbed his arm. "Let me go."

Ilsa watched Edric struggle with Gregor, Sofia ordering the noble to hold tight. The servants crouched at the timber stacked around her feet and struck flint to steel. She closed her eyes as flames flickered to life. It was so close. Would they still become human even if she died before the seven years were up? A dozen cries and the sound of wings made her eyes open.

Her brothers swooped in, attacking the servants, trying to put out the flames. She wanted to beg them to fly as far away as possible. Escape.

"Kill them," Sofia screeched. "I told you they'd come and save her. Now tell me she's not a witch."

Ilsa shook her head, wishing her hands were free so she could chase her brothers away. Gregor let Edric go and reached for his bow, sending an arrow flying in her direction.

Edric grabbed the bow from Gregor. "You'll kill her. What are you trying to do? Don't fire towards her." He threw the bow away and started towards Ilsa.

Gregor rushed after him, wrestling him to the ground while Sofia continued to throw orders around.

The flames grew higher and Ilsa felt the heat increase. She pressed her lips together, determined not to make a single sound. She wanted to close her eyes so she didn't see the moment the flames reached her, but her eyes refused to cooperate. The sun reached the horizon and Ilsa began to hope she might last the seven years.

Sofia strode towards her, a stick in her hand as she struck out at the ravens that tried to pull timber from the pyre. "Evil, unnatural creatures." The stick struck one of the ravens, knocking him to the ground.

Ilsa opened her mouth to scream, barely managing to stop herself in time. Tears streamed down her face and she strained against the ropes that held her. She stared at the raven lying completely still on the ground, almost certain it was Fredrick.

Flames licked at the hem of her dress as the curse broke and Aaron appeared in front of her. "Ilsa, you should have run. Why do you never run?" He batted at the flames with his hands.

Benjamin ran towards them, holding a knife, Edric beside him. Isaac grabbed hold of Sofia, dragging her towards the pyre. Two more of his brothers helped him while others grabbed Gregor and one checked Fredrick who continued to lie still.

As soon as the ropes were cut from her wrists, Aaron dragged Ilsa from the pyre. Sobbing, she threw her arms around her brother before letting go of him to run to Fredrick's side. Unused to speaking, she shook him, mentally begging him to open his eyes. When he did, she threw herself across his chest.

"You trying to finish off the job that witch did with her stick?" Fredrick gently pushed her away from him so he could sit up.

Ilsa smiled, tears still falling. Behind her she heard screaming and turned to see Sofia tied to the stake and several of her brothers restraining Edric. Gregor was out cold on the ground. It wasn't long before Sofia's screams ended and the flames leapt up higher, obscuring her body.

"Quiet." Aaron stood in front of the pyre, his hand pointed towards it. "We listened and watched as that witch plotted and planned to kill our sister. She was the true witch around here with her potions that caused illness and her men who burnt the village and her whisperings to the priest."

Edric stopped struggling. "You must be mistaken." His words sounded uncertain.

Aaron shook his head. "I am never mistaken when it comes to looking after my family." He pointed at Gregor. "Ask him when he comes to. Your mother paid him to leave and then she paid him to return."

Ilsa rose to her feet, crossing the courtyard to stand in front of Edric. She held out her hand to him.

Edric looked from Aaron to Ilsa, stepping forward to wrap his arms around her and crush her to him. "I'm sorry. I didn't know they were your brothers. I didn't know my mother was plotting against you. Can you ever forgive me?"

Ilsa looked up at him and smiled. "Yes." The word was a whisper. Speaking felt strange after being silent for so long.

Edric stared down at her. "You spoke. You can speak?"

Ilsa laughed, the sound louder than her first word.

Then everyone tried to talk at once. Benjamin and Isaac both trying to tell Edric how much Ilsa had endured to save them from the spell. Aaron finally roared 'quiet' and proceeded to briefly explain everything. Edric asked a lot of questions and eventually they all went inside and Benjamin prepared dinner with Ilsa's help.

By the time they retired for the night, Gregor in the dungeon and Ilsa's brothers in several guest rooms, Ilsa was still smiling. She could hardly believe it was all over and her brothers were human again.

Edric stopped at the door of their room, turning to Ilsa. "I never thought I'd hear you speak. It's a miracle."

"You can't imagine how often I wanted to speak. So many times I nearly did. But I couldn't make a single sound without causing my brothers' deaths."

"I'm sorry I didn't make it easy, especially these last few months."

Ilsa reached for him, her hand against his cheek. "You didn't know. And even not knowing, you were still willing to almost ruin your kingdom for me and my ravens."

"How could I not? You captured my heart the day I first met you. I would do anything for you."

"Anything?"

He took her hand and raised it to his lips. "Anything."

"How about helping my brothers win back their kingdom?"

Edric laughed. "Once my army has returned."

"Really?" She could hardly believe he'd agreed.

"I owe your father for sending that witch after you."

Ilsa smiled. "I'm actually sometimes grateful for that except for what my brothers endured. Without her I'd never have met you."

Edric drew her close, his arms holding her tight. "For that I'll let him live. For the witch I'll give his kingdom to Aaron."

Ilsa's laughter was cut off by Edric's kiss as she slid one arm around his neck, the other around his waist, holding him as tightly as he held her.

Free Ebook

Subscribe to Avril's newsletter and receive a free ebook. This ebook is exclusive to those on her mailing list. To find out more about this offer visit:

www.avrilsabine.com/free-ebook

*

information is confidential and you are under no obligation to remain on the mailing list and can unsubscribe at any time.

To The Reader

If you enjoyed this book, why not consider leaving a review to help other readers discover it too? Reader engagement is one of the few ways that lets an author know readers want more books in a particular series or genre. So leave a review and tell friends, not only about this book but also about other ones you've enjoyed, so you can continue to enjoy books by your favourite authors for years to come.

Dreams are meant to be lived,

Avril.

About The Author

Avril is an Australian author who lives with her family on acreage in South East Queensland. She writes mostly young adult and children's speculative fiction, but has been known to dabble in other genres. You can find more information about her at www.avrilsabine.com where you can also subscribe to her newsletter to be kept informed about new releases, current projects, blog posts and exclusive news.

Titles By Avril Sabine

Stories about strong characters and characters who discover their strengths.

SERIES

Assassins Of The Dead- Young Adult Fantasy/Paranormal

Book 1: Dark Blade

Book 2: Dragon Touched

Book 3: Society Against Vampires

Book 4: King's Request

Dragon Blood- Young Adult Urban Fantasy (with elements of romance)

(5 book series)

Book 1: Pliethin

Book 2: Wyvern

Book 3: Surety

Book 4: Knight

Book 5: Mage

Dragon Mage- Young Adult Urban Fantasy (with elements of romance)

(Series two of Dragon Blood series)

Book 1: Promise

Dragon Blood Chronicles- Young Adult Urban Fantasy (with elements of romance)

(Companion stand alone series to Dragon Blood)

Book 1: Oath

Book 2: Betrayed

Guardians Of The Round Table- Young Adult Fantasy LitRPG

(Co-written with Storm and Rhys Petersen)

Book 1: Dexterity Fail

Book 2: Goblin Boots

Book 3: Singed Feathers

Book 4: Frog Mage

Book 5: Crystal Mine

Book 6: Cursed Harp

Book 7: Treasure Seeker

Rosie's Rangers- Young Adult Western Steampunk

(6 book series)

Book 1: Justice

Book 2: Vengeance

Book 3: Treachery

Book 4: Accused

Book 5: Wanted

Book 6: Corruption

Mark Of Kings- Children's Fantasy

(Upper middle grade/preteen)

(4 book series)

Book 1: The Arena

Book 2: The Island

Book 3: The Assassin

Book 4: The King

STAND ALONE SERIES

Demon Hunters- Young Adult Urban Fantasy/Horror (with elements of romance)

Book 1: Blood Sacrifice

Book 2: Retribution

Book 3: Tainted

Book 4: Premonition

Book 5: Cursed

Book 6: Feud

Book 7: Extrication

Plea Of The Damned- Young Adult Urban Fantasy/Paranormal

(6 book series)

Book 1: Forgive Me Lucy

Book 2: Forgive Me Aiden

Book 3: Forgive Me Jena

Book 4: Forgive Me Kobe

Book 5: Forgive Me Marti

Book 6: Forgive Me Dawson

Realms Of The Fae- Young Adult Urban Fantasy (with elements of romance)

The Sword (short story in Like A Girl Anthology)

Heart Of Stone

Book 1: A Debt Owed

Book 2: Marked By The Hunt

Book 3: The Magic Collector

Book 4: An Unexpected Betrayal

Book 5: Imprisoned By Iron

Fairytales Retold (Short Stories)

Snow-White And Rose-Red

The Twelve Brothers

The Light Princess

Beauty And The Beast

Sleeping Beauty

Aschenputtel

The Golden Bird

The Frog Prince

The Death Of Koshchei The Deathless

Myths And Legends Retold (Short Stories)

Ion, Son Of Apollo

Sir Gawain And The Maid With The Narrow Sleeves

Princess Ilse, The Giant's Daughter

YOUNG ADULT NOVELS

Young Adult Fantasy (with elements of romance)

Elf Sight

Earth Bound

Young Adult Urban Fantasy

Stone Warrior (with elements of romance)

The Jungle Inside

Young Adult Contemporary (with elements of romance)

Through Your Eyes

The Ugly Stepsister

Perfect Little Princess

Young Adult Contemporary/ Paranormal

Whispers In The Dark (with elements of romance and same sex relationships)

Over Too Soon (with elements of romance)

Young Adult Sci-Fi

Experiment X-One-Six (Urban Sci-Fi/Superheroes)

An Endless Dawn (Post Apocalyptic Sci-Fi)

CHILDREN'S BOOKS

Dragon Lord (Preteen/early teens) (Fantasy)

The Irish Wizard (Upper middle grade) (Urban Fantasy)

SHORT STORIES

Urban Fantasy

Eternally Late

Dealings With Joe

Glimpses (short story in That Moment When Anthology)

Contemporary

The Brat Next Door

Fantasy LitRPG

(Set in the same world as Guardians Of The Round Table Series)

Tales Of Inadon 1: The Disc (Co-written with Storm and Rhys Petersen) (short story in Game On! Anthology)

Post Apocalyptic Sci-Fi

Compulsive Directive

NONFICTION

A Year Of Weekly Writing Exercises (Creative Writing)

Cooking For Families With Allergies (Cooking) (Co-written with Storm Petersen)

Tell Me A Story, Grandma (Memoir)

For the most up to date details on available titles visit:

www.avrilsabine.com/books/bibliography

Disclaimer

This is a work of fiction. Names, characters, businesses, places, events and incidents are either the products of the author's imagination or used in a fictitious manner. Any resemblance to actual persons, living or dead, or actual events is purely coincidental. The opinions expressed or beliefs held are those of the characters and should not be assumed to be the opinions or beliefs of the author.

9 781925 131444